Auss

Spider!

David Metzenthen

Illustrated by Peter Sheehan

Puffin Books

PUFFIN BOOKS

Published by the Penguin Group
Penguin Group (Australia)
250 Camberwell Road, Camberwell, Victoria 3124, Australia
(a division of Pearson Australia Group Pty Ltd)
Penguin Group (USA) Inc.
375 Hudson Street, New York, New York 10014, USA
Penguin Group (Canada)
10 Alcorn Avenue, Toronto, Ontario, Canada, M4V 3B2
(a division of Pearson Penguin Canada Inc.)
Penguin Books Ltd
80 Strand, London WC2R 0RL, England
Penguin Ireland
25 St Stephen's Green, Dublin 2, Ireland
(a division of Penguin Books Ltd)
Penguin Books India Pvt Ltd
11, Community Centre, Panchsheel Park, New Delhi-110 017, India
Penguin Group (NZ)
Cnr Airborne and Rosedale Roads, Albany, Auckland, New Zealand
(a division of Pearson New Zealand Ltd)
Penguin Books (South Africa) (Pty) Ltd
24 Sturdee Avenue, Rosebank, Johannesburg 2196, South Africa

Penguin Books Ltd, Registered Offices: 80 Strand, London WC2R 0RL, England

First published by Penguin Group (Australia), a division of
Pearson Australia Group Pty Ltd, 2004

3 5 7 9 10 8 6 4 2

Typeset in New Century School Book by Post Pre-press Group,
Brisbane, Queensland
Printed in Australia by McPherson's Printing Group,
Maryborough, Australia

Designed by Marina Messiha © Penguin Group (Australia)
Series designed by Melissa Fraser
Series Editor: Suzanne Wilson

National Library of Australia
Cataloguing-in-Publication data:

Metzenthen, David.
Spider!

ISBN 014 330099 7.

1. Spiders – Juvenile fiction. I. Sheehan, Peter, 1964- .
II. Title. (Series: Aussie bites).

A823.3

www.puffin.com.au

For Ella and Liam – *D.M.*

For Laura, the groover – *P.S.*

Chapter One

I saw the spider, and I
know the spider saw me.

'Yeee-*arkkkk*!' I yelled.
'Mum! There's a great big
huntsman spider in my
room. And I'm trapped!'

'Oh, that's nice, dear,'

Mum answered from the
sunroom. 'Just catch it, and
put it out in the park. It
will love all the new
gum trees.'

'No way!' I yelled. 'If you
want it, you catch it.'

My mum and dad are
members of the Protect Our
Parks and Wildlife Group.

3

They love all Australian plants and animals. And so do I, but not awfully big, *awfully* awful huntsman spiders!

Mum came in with a feather duster and a jar.

'I'll trap him, Min,' she said. 'And then we'll put him outside.'

'Make it snappy, please,' I said. 'Because I've got to go to school in twenty minutes.'

'I will do my best.' Mum showed the spider the duster. 'Now come here, Harold.'

I couldn't believe it. Mum had already given that *awful* spider a name!

Chapter Two

Mum stood on my bed.
Then she tried to shoo the
spider into the jar with the
duster. But the spider did
not want to be shooed. He
held on tight to my
certificate for riding the

Red Rocket roller coaster.

'Go into the jar please, Harold,' Mum said. 'There's a good boy.'

I wasn't so polite. 'Get in the jar, creepy!' I yelled.

'Get your own certificate!'

The spider let go with *some* of his legs. But he did not let go with *all* of his legs. So he stayed right where he was.

'We need someone taller,' Mum said. 'Get your dad to

bring in the broom, Min.'

I was not going *anywhere* near that spider. Spiders can jump. I've seen them. I stayed where I was.

'Dad!' I yelled. 'Bring the broom! There's a *spider* in here!'

Chapter Three

Dad brought the broom in and held it up.

'Here you go, Harold, old chap,' he said. 'Just climb on board and I'll carry you out to the new gum trees next door.'

'That's a good idea,' Mum said. 'Move the broom up close, dear. Then he'll step onto it. He knows we won't harm him.'

Dad put the broom next to Harold, but Harold took off like a frightened rabbit. He ran right up high and hid behind my dream catcher.

'I've got another idea,' I said. 'Why don't you just

give him a really good hard
whack? And turn him into
a spider pancake.'

'That's not very nice,
Min,' Dad said. 'He's
beautiful. Look at the
stripes on his legs.'

Ned, my older brother,
came into my room.

'Why don't you get the
vacuum cleaner?' he
suggested. 'And suck Hairy
Harry up the nozzle. Easy.'

'That's not a bad idea,'
Dad said.

'It's a very good idea,'
Mum said. 'I'll go and get it.'

Ned sat on the floor.

'I want to see this,' he said. 'Because I don't think *any* spider would like to be sucked up a vacuum cleaner.'

I thought Ned was right. For once.

Chapter Four

Dad held the vacuum
cleaner and stood on a
chair. Mum picked up the
broom to round Harold up.
Ned got ready to turn on
the power – and I got ready
to jump out the window,

in case things went terribly
wrong.

'Power on Low, Ned,' Dad
said quietly.

'POWER ON LOW!' Ned

yelled, and hit the switch.

Mum moved the broom towards Harold.

'Off you go, Harold,' she said. 'Toddle along, you

funny fellow. This won't
hurt a bit.'

But Harold did not toddle
along. As soon as the nozzle
got close he grabbed onto
one of my horse posters.

'Just a teensy weensy
little bit more power, Ned,'
Dad said.

'MORE POWER!' Ned
shouted, and turned the
power dial to Full.

All the hairs on Harold's

legs stood up. He looked
scared, but he did not let go.

'Tap him with the broom,'
Dad said to Mum. 'Loosen
his legs off.'

Mum tapped Harold, and
suddenly Harold disappeared
down the nozzle. I bet that
surprised him!

'*Brilliant!*' Mum cried. 'Oh, I hope Harold's all right in there.'

'He'll be fine.' Dad climbed down. 'By golly,' he added, 'that worked well.'

'It didn't just work *well*,' Ned said to Dad. 'It worked *fantastically!*'

'You reckon?' I said. 'Look who's coming back out to say hello.'

Chapter Five

We watched as Harold
climbed out of the vacuum
cleaner. He looked tired
and dusty.

'Boy, he must be strong,'
Ned said. 'I had the power
cranked up to ten.'

Harold stood on the carpet on his eight wobbly legs.

'Poor old Harold!' Mum said, talking to him on her hands and knees. 'You must've got a big fright.'

I picked up my school
bag. One false move and I
was ready to squash him.

'He's faking it,' I said.
'He'll jump at any second.'

Dad looked at his watch.

'Min,' he said, 'school starts

in seven minutes. Don't you have to take some *thing* along for World Environment Day?'

Dad was right. Then I got what he meant.

'All right, I'll take Harold,' I said, thinking hard. 'But only if he's in a really *tight* container with ten *thick* rubber bands.'

I had come up with a sneaky plan.

When Environment Day was over, I'd get one of the boys to take Harold to the other side of Highwood Highway. No spider could ever get back across six lanes of traffic and a tramline. Perfect.

Harold would be gone for ever!

Chapter Six

I went out the front gate
with Ned, and Harold who
was in an ice-cream
container in my bag.

'We'd better get some
bark,' Ned said. 'It must
be boring for him with

nothing to cling on to.'

Ned and I went into the park. Quickly we gathered some gum-tree bark and leaves. I put the container down.

'You take off the lid,' I said. 'And if he tries anything, I'll bang him with this stick.'

Ned took off the rubber bands and slowly lifted the lid. I raised my stick.

'Be careful, Ned,' I said. 'He won't remember that we've been nice to him.'

That's why spiders make hopeless pets. They only ever care about themselves.

Ned peered into the
container.

'He's asleep,' he said.

And he was. Harold was
in the corner sleeping like a

baby. So, carefully, Ned and I tucked him in with leaves and bark and shut the lid.

'He seems all right for a spider,' Ned said.

'Yeah, he seems okay, I guess,' I said. 'I just hope he doesn't go mad at school.'

Ned looked at me. 'Or on the way to school.'

Chapter Seven

Harold did make it to
school – along with all the
other things kids brought
for World Environment
Day. Tim brought a
cockatoo feather. Eliza
brought a snake skin,

but nobody else brought a
spider!

'Please bring Harold the
Huntsman to the front,
Min,' said Miss Tweedle.
'He won't do anything
naughty, will he?'

I hoped not.

'I think he'll be good,' I said. 'He was asleep last time I looked. Anyway, my mum and dad said huntsman spiders are harmless.

Slowly I took off the lid –
but this time Harold was
wide awake. He scuttled
out so quickly I couldn't
stop him.

'*Eeeek!*' I dropped the
container.

Harold sprinted across
the floor. He looked
terrified. He was sucking on

a little gumnut as if it was
a dummy! Suddenly I felt
sorry for him – but Miss
Tweedle didn't. She picked
up her wooden ruler.

'Stand back, Min!' she said. 'I'm going to whack that DEADLY BEAST before it BITES someone!' And she chased poor Harold into the corner.

'No!' I yelled. 'Don't
whack him, Miss Tweedle!'
I took a big breath.
'I'll catch him,' I said.
Then I took an even
bigger breath – and I
swooped on Harold like
a police rescue helicopter!

I had saved his life.

'Take that monster outside,' Miss Tweedle said. 'You have one minute to get rid of it, Min. Or I will stamp on it myself.'

'Yes, Miss Tweedle,' I said, and out I went.

Chapter Eight

I knew I had only one
minute to get rid of Harold.
I would've put him into the
school garden, but there
are no gum trees for him.
And if I put him on the
oval, kids would jump on

45

him. I lifted the corner of
the lid.

Harold was holding onto
his last little piece of bark
as if it was a teddy bear.
He looked worried and
miserable. What could I do?
I knew that *I* didn't want
to squash him any more –
but I knew that Miss
Tweedle did!

I heard a spluttering
noise. It was the postman

on his motorbike stopping
at the school letterbox. I
had an idea.

I ran to the fence with
Harold's container. Behind

me I could hear Miss
Tweedle's heavy footsteps.

'Excuse me,' I said to the
postman. 'Could you please
take this spider to a place

with gum trees and let him out? It's a matter of life and death.'

'I'm coming for that monster!' Miss Tweedle yelled.

'He's only a harmless huntsman called Harold,' I told the postman. 'Miss Tweedle is going to stamp on him. *Please* save him.'

'No worries,' said the postman. 'I don't mind huntsmans. I'm from the bush!'

'Thanks,' I said, and handed over Harold's container.

The postman tucked it

in one of his letter bags.

'I'll take him to Lynden Gum Tree Park,' he said. 'It's two kilometres across Highwood Highway and one kilometre past Black Yabby Creek. Harold will love it there.'

'All right,' I said. 'Goodbye, Harold. I'll miss you.'

Boy, I never thought I'd say *that* to a spider!

And off Harold went, at
twenty kilometres an hour.

Chapter Nine

It's now one week since
World Environment Day
and I'm out in the backyard.
I ended up using a cocoon
for my environment project,
but it wasn't nearly as
interesting as Harold.

I miss him. I guess I'll never meet another spider as good as he was.

Suddenly something on
top of the fence catches
my eye. It has eight hairy
legs and is holding a little
piece of bark like a teddy

bear. And sucking on a gumnut like a dummy! 'Harold!' I yell. 'Oh, Harold. How did you get back here?'

Harold just looks at me.
He seems very tired. He
must've been walking for
days. He must've crossed
the highway, the tram

track, and Black Yabby
Creek. He's come back to
find me!

'Wait there for one
minute, Harold,' I say. 'I've
got to get you something!'

I rush inside and get an
ice-cream container. Then I
fill it with lovely bark and
leaves for a cosy bed. Then
I put Harold in, take him to
the park, and stick him up
a gum tree.

'There you go, Harold,' I say. 'Now you stay there.'

After all, I might not hate huntsman spiders any more – but that doesn't mean I want to have one living in my house!

From David Metzenthen

This story is based on a huntsman spider that I found at home. My children and I did catch it with the vacuum cleaner – and it *did* crawl back out! In the end, we put it way down in the garden, and never saw it again. Thank goodness!

From Peter Sheehan

I was scared of spiders till I really looked at them. My heart changed after I gained the courage to watch them build their webs, crawl and wait. They are so patient, so focused, so quietly amazing. None-the-less, I must admit, I still prefer it when they are amazing out in the garden!

Want another
nibble?

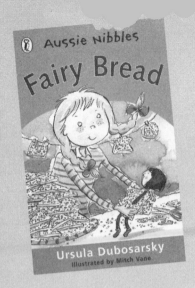

Becky only wants fairy bread at
her party. But there's so much left
over, and she won't throw it out.

Dad saves a scruffy little
dog from being run over.
But whose dog is it?

Anna had never slept over at a
friend's house. Until now . . .
Was she brave enough?

Susie is the shyest girl in
school, but she's got a secret.
A big one . . .